P9-AOR-816

This is a Dorling Kindersley Book
published by Random House, Inc.

Senior Editor Jane Yorke
Editor Charlotte Davies
Art Editor Toni Rann
Designer Heather Blackham
Photography Stephen Oliver
Additional photography Jerry Young
Series Consultant Neil Morris

First American edition, 1991

Published in the United States by Random House, Inc., New York.
This edition first published in Great Britain by
Dorling Kindersley Publishers Limited in 1991.

Library of Congress Cataloging-in-Publication Data
My first look at sorting.
p. cm.
Summary: Photographs of animal pairs, matching pairs, and
other kinds of groups introduce the concept of sorting.
ISBN 0-679-81162-1
1. Set theory – Juvenile literature. [1. Set theory.]
I. Random House (Firm) II. Title: Sorting.
QA248.M89 1991
511.3'22 – dc20
90-8575 CIP AC

Manufactured in Italy 2 3 4 5 6 7 8 9 10

Reproduced by Bright Arts, Hong Kong
Printed and bound in Italy by L.E.G.O.

· MY · FIRST · LOOK · AT ·

Sorting

Random House New York

Odd one out

Which button is a different color?

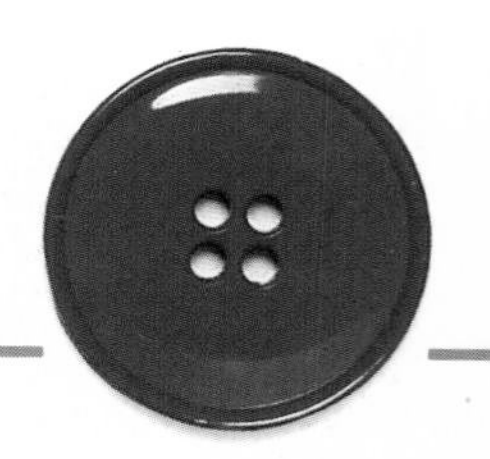

Which present
does not belong here?

In the right place

What does not belong in the garden?

parrot
elephant
giraffe
Which animal does not have a match?
lion
mouse

Matching pairs

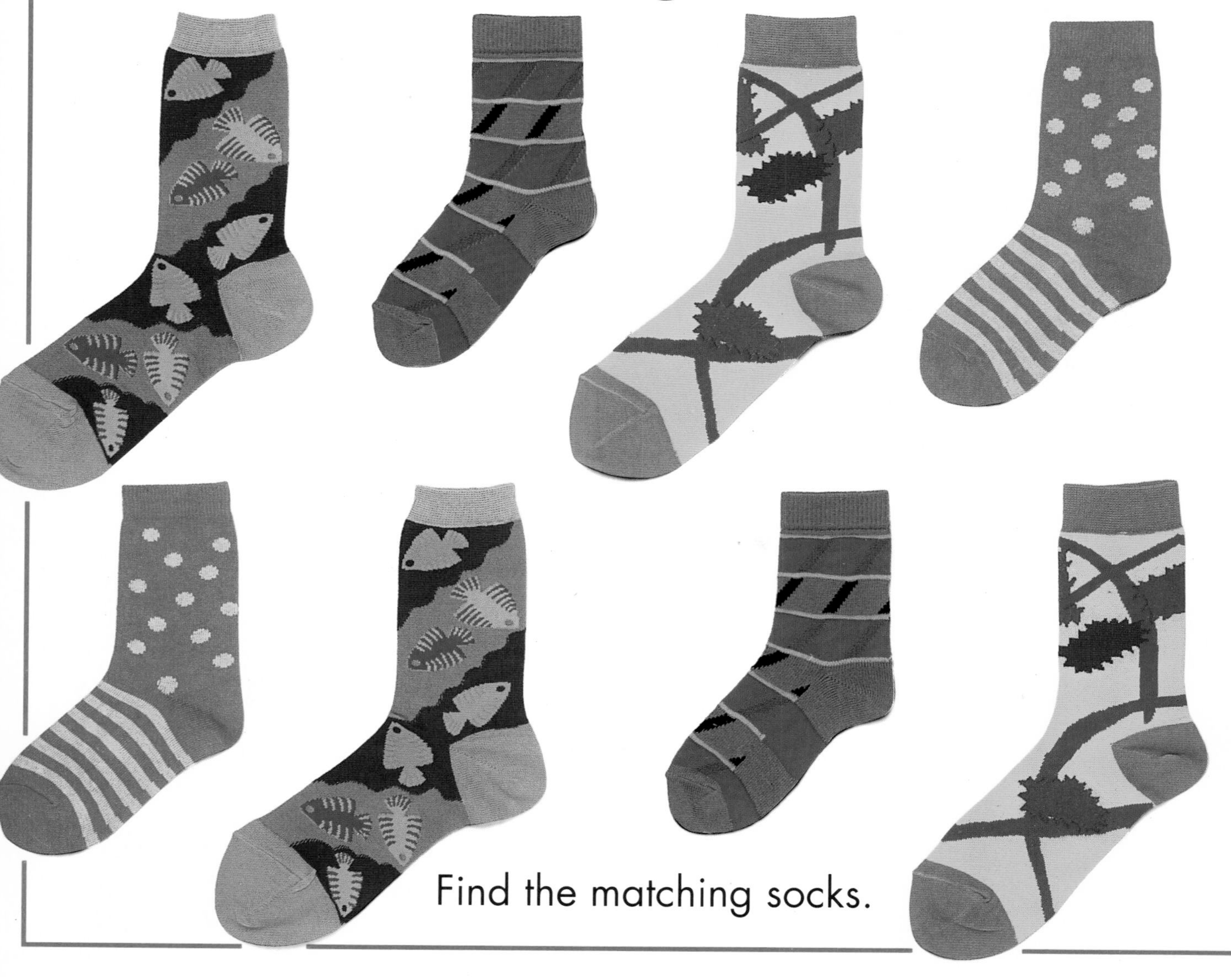

Find the matching socks.

Which shoes go together?

Sorting colors

Can you match each tractor to the right trailer?

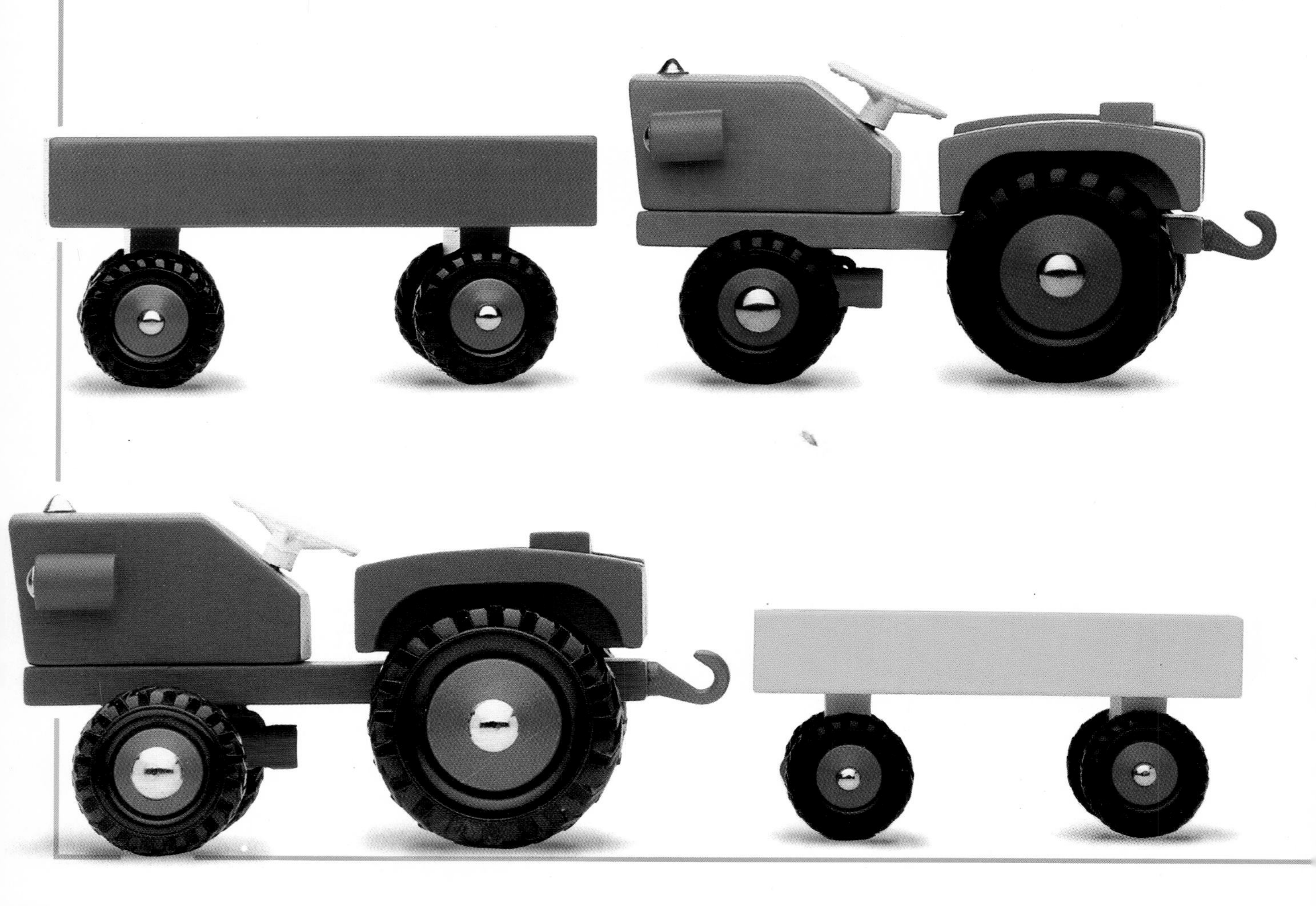

seeds
leaves
flowers
seed packet
clock
butterfly
bulbs

Animal pairs

Can you find the matching animal pairs?

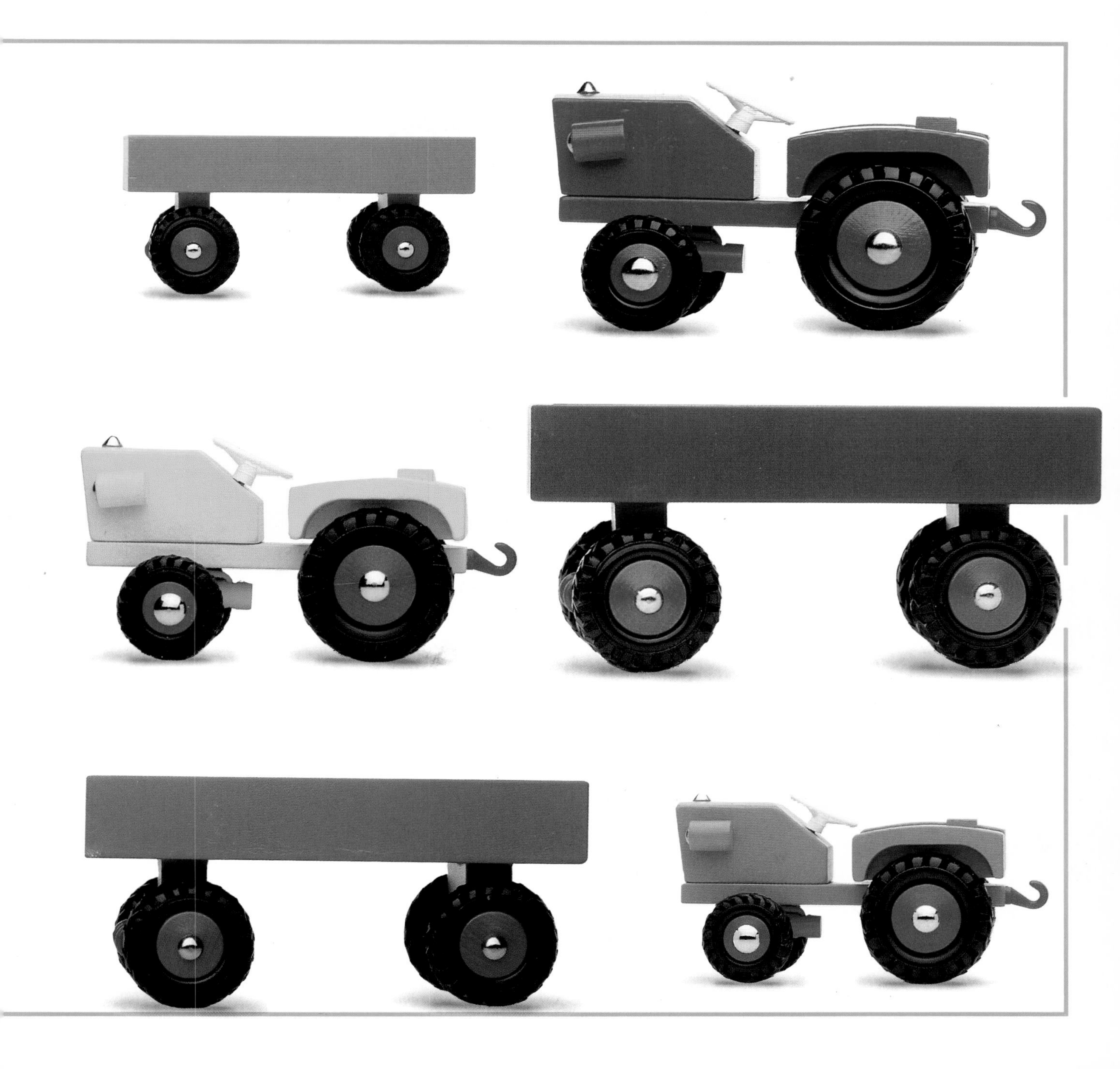

Sorting sizes

There are five jars of candy.

Which one is the biggest?

Which one
is the smallest?

Matching up

Do you know which things go together?

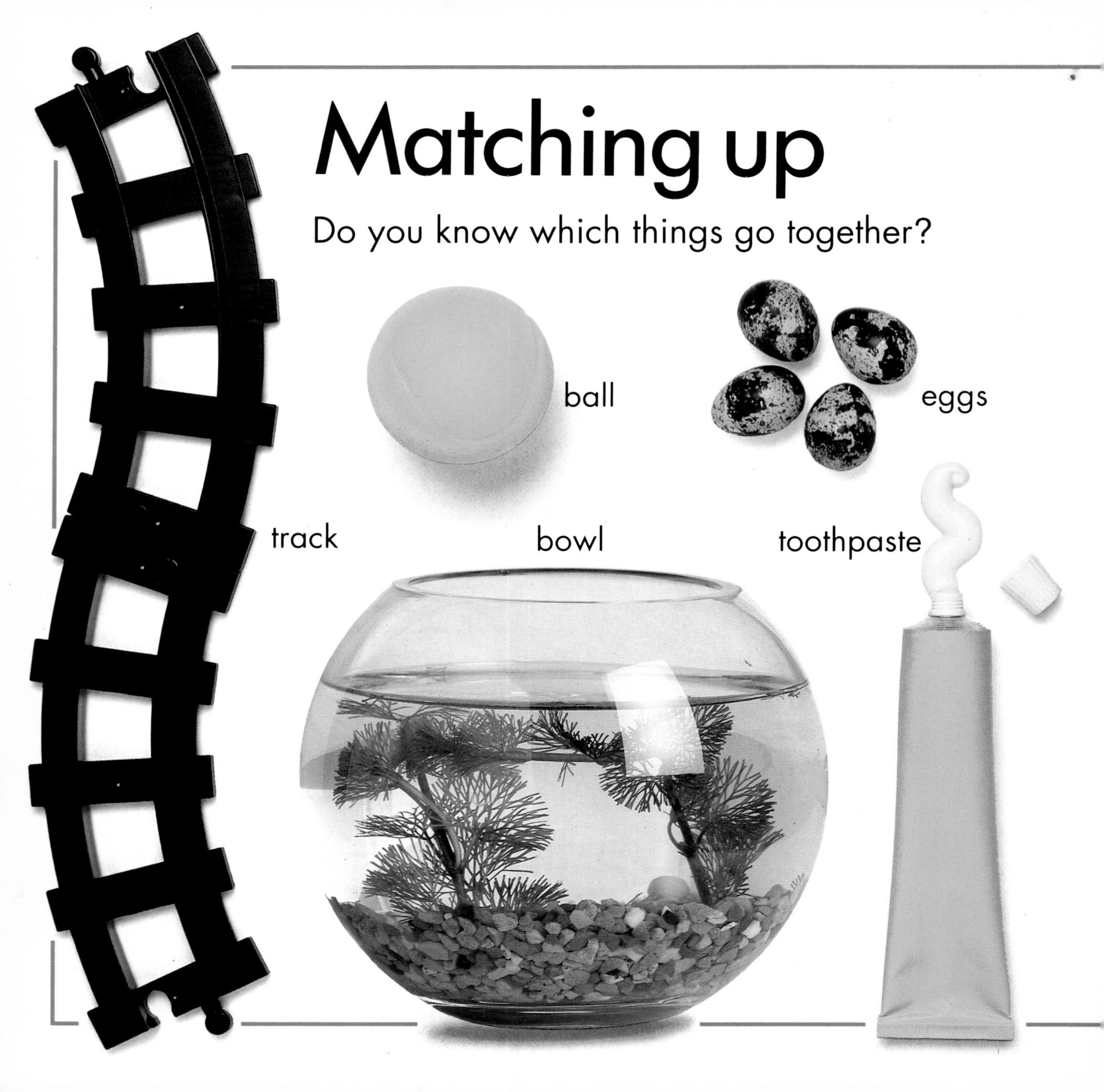

goldfish
nest
toothbrush
racket
train

All mixed up

Can you sort these toys and clothes into two groups?

pull toy

roller skates

T-shirt

scarf

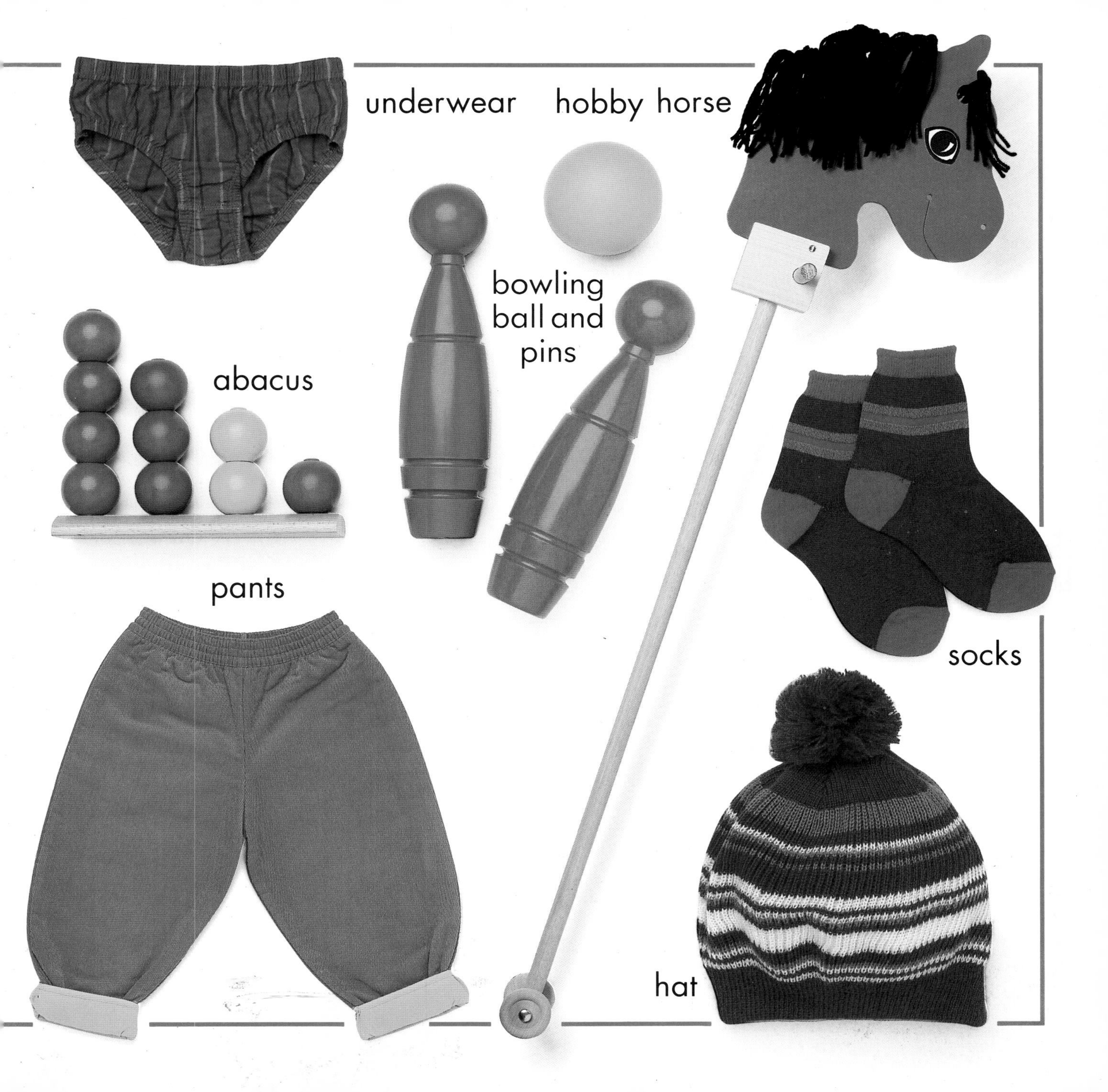
underwear
hobby horse
bowling ball and pins
abacus
pants
socks
hat